HarperCollins Children's Books is a division of HarperCollins Publishers Ltd.
Text and illustrations copyright © Rob Biddulph 2021
The author/illustrator asserts the moral right to be identified as the author/illustrator
of the work. A CIP catalogue record for this book is available from the British Library.
All rights reserved.

1 London Bridge Street, London SE1 9GF
HarperCollins*Publishers*, 1st Floor, Watermarque Building, Ringsend Road, Dublin 4, Ireland

Visit our website at www.harpercollins.co.uk

ISBN 978-0-00-841335-4
Printed and bound in China
1 3 5 7 9 10 8 6 4 2

Things to find in this book

Five gold rings ☐
Four calling birds ☐
Three French hens ☐
Two turtle doves ☐
A partridge in a pear tree ☐

AN ODD DOG CHRISTMAS

Written and illustrated by

Rob Biddulph

HarperCollins *Children's Books*

For festive dogs
a festive day.

It's Christmas Eve!
Hip hip hooray!

Singing!

Baking!

Wrapping!

Fun!

A merry time for everyone.

But wait. Look closer. Can you see
One dog behaving differently?

Someone on
this carousel

Is jingling a
different bell.

"I'm stumped," she sighs. "Confounded. Stuck.

I've shopped all day, but still no luck.

As Christmas Eve turns out its light,
She wanders through the silent night.

What's this?
A sign!
An arrow too!

STEP INTO
Christmas

She takes a breath

STEP INTO
Christmas

STEP INTO *Christmas*

SANTA'S GROTTO

"Well, bless my bones!
Is this a dream?

A winter wonderland
supreme!

With candy canes
and gingerbread...

And jolly elves
in green and red!"

But wait. Look closer. Can you see
Someone *not* feeling Christmassy?

A sniff. A cough. A loud "ATCHOO!".
This red-nosed reindeer's feeling... blue.

ATCHOO!

DASHER

"Poor thing," she says, "you don't look well.
You've got a sniffle – I can tell."

He blows his nose. He wipes his eyes.
"You're right," the poorly reindeer sighs.

"I hate to moan or cause a fuss
(Tonight's a special night for us)

But truth be told –" he turns away –
"I'm far too ill to pull the sleigh."

Her tummy flips.
Her belly flops.
"Tonight?
The sleigh?"
The penny drops.

They head back to the reindeer shed
And poor old Dasher goes to bed.

But then a warm voice, deep and clear,
Says...

"Welcome, friend.
I'm glad you're here."

"You see," declares the chap in red,
"We've got a busy night ahead.

And," says he, with worried frown,
"We are, it seems, a reindeer down..."

This dog, she does not hesitate.
She smiles a smile and stands up straight.

"I'm ready, Santa! What's the plan?
I'll help in any way I can."

And so, with Odd Dog flying high...

They blazed a trail across the sky

Their busy night is at an end
And Odd Dog's thoughts
turn to her friend.

Santa smiles. "Here's my advice:
While toys and games are very nice,

A simple present from the heart
Is always the best place to start."

And just like that,
it's crystal clear.

This dog has had
a great idea.

Caring, sharing, friendship, fun.

Merry Christmas, everyone!